LAND OF SAPPHIRE AND SAFFRON

KISHTWAR

BY

SHAFQAT SHEIKH

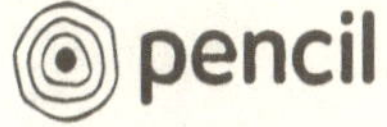

ISBN 978-93-5438-947-4

Published in India 2020 by Pencil

A brand of
One Point Six Technologies Pvt. Ltd.
123, Building J2, Shram Seva Premises,
Wadala Truck Terminal, Wadala (E)
Mumbai 400037, Maharashtra, INDIA
E connect@thepencilapp.com
W www.thepencilapp.com

Author biography

"Shafqat Sheikh, A young Freelancer from Bunjwah Kishtwar"

Hailing from a remote and past militancy hit Bunjwah region of Kishtwar district in Jammu and Kashmir, Shafqat Sheikh was born on 05 June 1994 in a middle poor class family at his native village Binoon of Tehsil Bunjwah in Kishtwar district. At the time of his birth and childhood, his family including his parents get harassed by various elements as militancy was on peak in the area and the family income was very low and was dependent on agricultural and other home practices. The parents of Shafqat were having a ray of hope among him as, He was first male child in their family and the grandparents had served him a lot at the time of his childhood. Since from the day of birth, Shafqat's life takes various U turns despite the parents were feeling unsafe and unsecure as they have faces various tortures from various ends.

Despite all these, When Shafqat was 4 years old had joined a private reputed institution 'Amin Academy Bunjwah' in 1998 in his neighbouring village Jawalapur where Shafqat received basic education from Nursery upto class 8th till 2008 and later joined government institution in 9th class upto 12th received education from Government Higher Secondary School Binoon till 2013. Continuing his studies, Shafqat joined Government Degree College Kishtwar in 2013 in Arts stream and unfortunately due to unfavourable circumstances of his family, He was unable to attend the exam of two subject that results his failure in examination and wastage of year in academic session during 2014.

Having ray of hope for betterment of life, Shafqat joined paramedical college in 2014 as Pharmacist trainee in Doda of which study centre was in kishtwar that later was shifted to Doda and passed the examination through Jammu and Kashmir State Paramedical Council Jammu in Dec 2017. During his training as Pharmacist, Shafqat also decided to continue his studies through distance mode via IGNOU and completed Graduation in year 2018 in Arts stream.

During the spans of life in 2013, Shafqat's life feels disgraced when Shafqat applied for post of teacher through RET mode in School Education Department that the post was later changed as General line teacher to provide undue benefits to some blue-eyed persons. Having not any political or economicalmilage, Shafqat can't challenge the orders passed by Education Department. The rejection of name in panel changes mind not to lose hope but to do so that everyone could ask you for help to curb such injustice with others that happens with Shafqat.

During the time, Shafqat was using social networking sites including facebook through which Shafqat get connected with one of the dynamic Journalist Mohd Majid Malik who via his telephonic call published a news story of Bunjwah using his reference in the story, that was second time Shafqat's name was published in newspaper and He get too much excited after reading his name in newspaper for that, He received various appreciations from various corners. The news story changes his mind to become journalist and voice of voiceless. The day was a historic day in Shafqat's life when a news was carried in reputed newspaper by tagline and finally Shafqat worked as Reporter of Newspaper till 2015 under the able guidance of Sr. Journalists Mohd Majid Malik, Junaid Malik, Mansoor Qadir, and various others.

Although working as Reporter, one day when a news items was not carried by reputed Newspaper, Shafqat decided to write voluntarily and to be a Freelancer. Working as Freelance Journalist, Shafqat got various opportunities but finally decided to be a freelancer and to became an independent voice of voiceless. Since from 2016, Shafqat writes various news stories and raised various issues across Chenab Valley through print and electronic media as Freelancer. Shafqat writes hundreds of columns, articles and editorials that gets published in various leading dailies, weeklies Newspaper of state and even in National Newspapers.

During the time working as Freelancer and advantages of social networking sites, Shafqat gets membership in All Indian Reporters Association as State Secretary from Jammu and Kashmir, and later in Human Right Organizations that backed up him in raising the issues on public interest from 2015. In 2017 Shafqat's name was shortlisted for 'Voice of Kashmir Journalist of year Award' from National Human Right Social Justice Commission New Delhi by Amb. Amar Sarang. But unfortunately, Shafqat failed to attend the award ceremony due to his unfavourable circumstances of his personal issues in family. Continuing working as Freelancer, 'French Club Jammu' features Shafqat Sheikh as 'Personality of Jammu' and awarded him Journalist of the Year award on 15 Mar 2019 that encourages his hopes and helps in writing columns and articles on public interest. Impressed with raising the public issues and working on public interest, India Star Book of Records, INDIA STAR ICON AWARD 2019, shortlisted Shafqat's name as best awardee in field of 'Social Activism and Journalism' of which all awardee certificates and badges were received via courier as Shafqat was stucked off in Kishtwar where section 144 was imposed and internet was snapped by District Administration Kishtwar facing law and order situations across Kishtwar.

Not only this Shafqat bagged AN CONSULTANCY INDIA FMBAF (Film Media Business Academy

Fashion) prestigious Award for his outstanding performance in Social Works across Jammu and Kashmir. The award ceremony was held on 13 Jun 2019 at St Andrews Auditorium Bandra West Mumbai Maharashtra where Shafqat was awarded with 24 krat Gold plated Award Certificate and AN Consultancy India Gold plated Medal.

Having interest in Journalism, Shafqat seeks admission in PG Course in Journalism and Mass Communication through IGNOU of which yet Shafqat pursuing studies.

Beside all this Shafqat was awarded as Best Reporter Award by NSS Unit of GDC Kishtwar in collaboration of District Administration Kishtwar for mass awareness of Beti Bachao Beti Padhao and SVEEP campaign during 2019 and also bagged best Columnist Award on occasion of Republic Day 2020 by District Administration Kishtwar. Shafqat was also felicitated by French Club Jammu during International Players Meet Up 2020 held at Sweet Temptation inside Maharaja Hari Singh Jammu on 15 Mar 2020.

Shafqat also gets Corona Warrior Certificate from LAZAWAL, for his tireless effort during Covid-19 lockdown. Shafqat also bagged I Can Foundation Humanitarian Excellence Award 2020 for his best Reporting and Activism for betterment of the society.

During the time of reporting and raising the issues on public interest, Shafqat received various threats, emotional tortures and family blackmailing from various corners but By Almighty Allah blessing no one can stop me and even my father was harassed by various goons to stop me from raising the issues of common masses.

Now a days, Journalism had become may passion and profession for providing helping hands among all needy and orphans as through various organisations including Global Peace Foundation, Khidmat Foundation and SHAHEEN Trust, I am providing helping hands for all masses without any discrimination of caste or religion.

Shafqat said that my shorter span of life changes my mind to become voice of voiceless and is trying to become one who win the heart of others despite that "Only Death can Silent me else No One can face Me".

Contents

Introduction 11

Leadership crisis leading to alienation 12

Socio-Ecnomic Background 17

Political Figure 27

"Education in Kishtwar" 30

"Healthcare and Medical Aid system in Kishtwar" 33

"View Point" 38

Introduction

This book titled the name "Kishtwar, Land of Saffron", is in your hands in which the author tries to bring the unexplored region, that became victim and prey of politicians, terrorists, blackmailers who try to destroy the long decade's peaceful atmosphere and to create hurdles in developmental works on socio-economical backwardness.

The book is dedicated to all accidental victims who lost their precious lives on Batote Kishtwar 244 National Highway and inter-district routes of Kishtwar district. These accidental victims had become prey of so-called political leaders who had done nothing but played with precious and innocent lives.

The aim of the author is to start a mass movement and awareness among the general public to fight for their own rights and to create a bond of friendship, brotherhood among all communities without any caste, creed, color, religion.

Shafqat Sheikh

Freelance

Journalist Columnist

Leadership crisis leading to alienation

History stands testimony to the fact that any nation has risen in the world to hey of its civilisation apart from other factors due to the acumen and quality of leadership it nurtures which in turn proves a source of the spa to the developing nation.

It is the leadership of a nation that have given ideologies and materialised them and few among them are Mao, Stalin, Hitler, Napoleon etc. among whom few are considered devils and some demi-gods by their respective people but one thing common among them was at least that they were faithful to their own people.

It is really ironical that the phase through which country is going will only produce corrupt, self-centred and epitome of violators and exploiters. The inability and lack of will among the so-called leadership of the country has even torn apart the social fabric of the society devoicing it of all the morals and moors of a civilised society. Bringing it much closer to our homeland of Jammu and Kashmir it seems the leadership here, since its inception on so-called democratic and secular front from the monarchical phase has only produced impotent lascivious and centre appeasing leadership which has brought alienation and hatred among the masses more particularly among the youth. The frustration is clearly depicted on the streets of Kashmir. This self-centric approach of our leadership has failed to make any progress on the social and economic front since decades sandwiched with broken promises, backstabbing. The prevalent carrot and rod policy harbour a deep sense of alienation and trust deficit among the masses.

The biggest problem here is that our leadership is just a puppet dancing to the tunes of the centre albeit this concern has been voiced by so many other states especially the southern ones regarding their cultural and linguistic invasion by an alien culture from outside, but the problem here particularly is that our leaders have always voluntarily gone to them with bent knees and folded hands to come to this chaste land of Sufis and saints to spill the blood of common people so as to remain in power corridors. This factual position is evident from the chronicles of history right from 1947 more explicitly and more clearly. The history is inundated with the fact that our own men have been the front runners to put in draconian laws like POTA, AFSPA and so many others even before they were implemented in any other part of India. The lack of belongingness and affinity of our leaders towards their homeland has let others to plunder our wealth, our honour and our unique cultural ethos.

It is important to mention here that our own people in the form of these leaders have given birth to renegades and so many such agencies wherein they were used to kill their own kith and kins enjoying the patronage of the colonial state and even decorated with honours and rewards.

Our state leadership is at war with its own people as thousands of teenagers, young and even old and women are languishing in jails since they raised their voice for their rights. If one may take in to account the turn of events only since 1947 after India attained the independence, one can easily see the atrocities committed by our state leaders to whatever group or political party they belonged to; their power-hungry hands are still oozing with the innocent blood of our brothers. Our state leadership in order to remain in power has sold their conscious a number of times may it in 1953, 1959, 1965, 1971, 1986 through different accords and agreements better to be called as a sell-out of Kashmir. Article 370 giving special status to the state of Jammu and Kashmir has now become irrelevant and has been made porous to the most possible extent.

The Hindu nationalistic forces including BJP and like groups need not to raise their clamours to make this law null and void since this chaste work has already been done by our beloved leaders of the state. Apart from the political front, the gruesome acts committed in the pure land of Kashmir including Kunan-Poshpora, Shopian, Chiittisinghpora are few among the million incidents that have been committed by inimical forces. Even after these inhuman and cruel acts none of our men has ever dared to raise the voice of their brethren but they have done worth mentioning is that of legitimising these acts just to remain in power and to please their mentors sitting in Delhi Darbar.

The gruesome incidents of Gool and subsequently that of Kishtwar in which people were killed and burnt alive are just a tip of the iceberg since this has been happening even before the day of July 1931. The blood of Kashmir has always been used to nurture the gardens of treacherous leaders. They might have their birth lineage connected to Kashmir but they were always alien towards to its soil and its people. The nation here will never forgive the treachery they have committed with the peace-loving people of this township.

The streets in Kashmir will always see a grieved alienated common man with the most lethal weapon in the world "a stone" to protect his honour, the dignity of his sisters and mothers against the colonial rule. The blood of innocent people will keep on writing the chronicles of Kashmir history squeezed out by its own leadership. This hatred and alienation among the masses is the sole source of these slave leaders to keep the pot boiling so as to earn their livings on the graves of their own sons and daughters. We as a nation must rise must awake so as to free ourselves from the clutches of these people lest we may pass the same heritage of slavery and bondage to our coming generations.

Socio-Ecnomic Background

Kishtwar District is a newly formed district of the state of Jammu and Kashmir. As of 2011, it is the third least populous district of Jammu and Kashmir (out of 22), after Kargil and Leh. Consisting of 13 blocks: Marwah, Warwan, Dacchan, Kishtwar, Nagseni, Drabshalla, Inderwal, Chatroo, Bunjwah, Trigam, Thakrie, Mughal Maidan, and Padder.

The Chenab River flows through the district. Major Hydel power projects in Kishtwar are DulHasti, Kirthai, Pakal Dool, Lower Kalnai, Rattle Power Project. The Sapphire is produced from a single mine at Padder valley. There is a gypsum mine at Trigram. The Steep Brahma mountain peak is situated at Dachan. Saffron of purest quality is produced in iron-rich soil at Pocchal, Matta, Lachdayaram, and Hidyal. Kishtwar National Park in the northeast region of the district has a large number of peaks and glaciers. District Kishtwar in the past used to be an independent hill principality the present name, related to "Kishat Rishi" who stayed here, is the modified version of the earlier name of Kishaswar.

Located about 238 km from Jammu at a height of 5,360 feet, Kishtwar in its ancient form Kashthavata is first referred to in the Rajatarangini during the reign of Raja

Kalsa of Kashmir (1063–1089), when "Uttamaraja", the ruler of Kashthavata visited the court of Kashmiri king in company with several other hill chiefs to pay their respects to the Raja. The Mehta Family was gifted the lands of Kishtwar by the King of Kashmir. Their family temple "Hatta Wali Mata" and their Heritage can still be tracked back to Kishtwar. The founder of this family was the Commander-in-Chief of the Kashmir Army "Sip-E-Salar Sri Jiya Lal Mehta". Known for his Bravery and valor he fought the Mughals and Northern raiders who invaded the land.

"Kishtwar", A famous township in Chenab valley having its own status and representation in the Union Territory of Jammu and Kashmir remains neglected from Independent India. Having hub of tourism, natural beauties, meadows, springs, forests, rivers, etc, in which SinthanTop, Chowgan ground, Devigol Bunjwah, and Bimal Nag Saroor are among of them. Besides natural beauties, the Chenab river flowing from the same district toward winter capital city and over which various Hydro Electric Power Projects has been constructed and some are under construction. The township was popularly known as "Valley of Saffron" in Chenab Valley of Jammu and Kashmir Union Territory had created a history of brotherhood and humanity during the past few decades when the whole country was in the turmoil of militancy and terrorism. In past, Kishtwar witnessed various ups and downs among various sectors, but it was our ancestors who always keep the torch of humanity glowing and had created a history of brotherhood across the whole region.

The remote town in Jammu and Kashmir that has been in the news for communal violence from past, till two decades back Kishtwar was known for its inter-community relations. The common refrain here used to be the exemplary situation in 1947 when conscious collective efforts were made by the elders of both the Hindu and Muslim communities to maintain the mutual trust that existed between them. While communal riots took place elsewhere in Jammu and in the nearby towns of Bhaderwah and Bhalessa, Kishtwar remained totally unaffected. So safe was this town that Muslims from other parts of the region sought refuge here and continued to live here. The town that forms the district headquarters (the district of Kishtwar was carved out of Doda district in 2006) represents a mosaic of religious, linguistic, and social identities and is known not only for its inclusive social and cultural life but also for shreds religious spaces.

"I came to know that a mass leader and Prime Minister of India Ms. Indra Gandhi visited Kishtwar and laid the foundation stone of Dul Hasti Power Project in 19th century". From the day many ups and downs came in Kishtwar as this township remain highly sensitive during the militancy period. In the same case, this township was once again under the pressure of terrorists,s and this beautiful valley changes from tourism to terrorism during the past few decades.

As the past happening is unknown to the author but a little bit of information received while having interaction with ancestors that in the valley of Kishtwar, A famous religious and spiritual figure "Shah Farid-Ud-Din Bagdadi" came from Bagdad and settled here and later was buried in Kishtwar for which Kishtwar valley became a most famous region in Jammu and Kashmir. "The patron saint of Kishtwar is Hazrat Shah Farid-Ud-Din Baghdadi — a Sufi saint who is known to have spread Islam in this area whose shrine is revered equally by Muslims and Hindus. Local narratives about the saint, especially those told by Hindus, have a special mention for his Hindu Rajput wife and the reverence they have for her. Also revered is his son, Hazrat Shah Asrar-Ud-Din Baghdadi, who is said to have miraculously revived his Hindu friend after he had died". Being part of a backward district, people here have been united in their varied struggles. One of the prominent places of the town is a memorial with three graves and two samadhis. Five students three Muslims and two Hindus were killed in the early 1980s while agitating for a college. People here have also collectively agitated for district status for Kishtwar.

Having such figures in Kishtwar, this township remains neglected by political parties and politicians for the last several years. Having the status of the district and two Assembly constituencies, this township became the prey of politicians and remains far away from development. Kishtwar the land of saffron, sapphire, and shrines was an independent hilly state during the medieval period when Maharaja Gulab Singh, the Dogra ruler of Jammu annexed it in 1821 AD. District Kishtwar was carved out from the erstwhile District Doda during the year 2007-08 when the Chief Minister of the state Jammu and Kashmir Shri Ghulam Nabi Azad had taken a historic decision for the creation of the new district. It has the unique distinction of being one of the biggest districts of the UT in the area just next to Leh and Kargil districts. Its area is almost one-half of the total area of eleven districts of the valley and one-third of the area of the Jammu region which too has eleven districts.

Inter-community relations started changing in Kishtwar in the early 1990s. This was the period when militancy entered the district of Doda. The vastness of the district, with a difficult mountainous terrain and villages located in remote areas, provided a safe haven to militants. The demography of the district also provided them a reason to base themselves here. Though the concerns of the district remained different, the ethnic Kashmiri Muslim population of the district (mostly migrants from adjacent areas of Kashmir) generally sympathized with the politics of the valley. That is the reason why, to begin with, there was local recruitment to militancy as well. However, gradually, foreign jihadis started outnumbering the local militants and the response of the people towards militancy also started changing. Militancy created its own kind of divide between the communities. The Muslim population got struck between the militants and the security forces. They were compelled to cater to the demands of the militants, mostly of food and shelter, and were thereafter also pressured by the security forces. The violence that was perpetrated during this period created the first seeds of mistrust between the communities, though intercommunity relations were not as much affected even at that time.

History, geography, topography, demography, area, and population define the status of a place or region. Kishtwar is almost mountainous like that of the Himachal or Ladakh region. District Kishtwar has its boundaries touching the valleys of Himachal in the southeast and Doda on the South-West. The entire district is full of mountains, forest,s, and hills. Hindus, Muslims, and Sikhs all reside here with peace, amity, and brotherhood. He advised the people of Kishtwar to follow the lofty ideas and preaching of saints, seers, and peers for which Kishtwar is well known and famous for and not to fall prey to the hate speeches and malicious propaganda of few anti-social elements existing in the society. This was reflected as early as 1993 when there was the first outbreak of communal tension. Since then, there have been some minor frictions but also some major violent clashes, as in 2003 and 2008. A few shops were burnt and some people were injured in 2003, but in 2008 two people were killed. Even though militancy has declined, communal sensitivities continue to be exploited by political actors. Over time, rightist politics and fundamentalist forces have gained much space. Jamaat-e-Islami and RSS have created exclusive constituencies of Muslims and Hindus. Working on these exclusive constituencies, almost all the political parties operating in the area, including, the Bhartiya Janta Party, National Conference Indian National Congress, and Peoples Democratic Party, find it convenient to mobilize support by playing on the fears and mutual suspicions. That results in Kishtwar becoming the prey of politicians for their pity gain. Some regions of Kishtwar peoples living there are surviving without any caste, creed, color, and religion, as they are being deprived of basic rights and await basic amenities. The regions including Marwah, Dacchan, Warwan, Bunjwah are not having road connectivity and have to shoulder patients and pregnant ladies to reach District Hospital Kishtwar from where we have to lift them to Government Medical College Jammu.

"Roads are called the backbone of development, Unfortunately, Marwah Dacchan Warwan, Kither is still not connected with District Headquarter Kishtwar and rest with State by road connectivity as the work was started in a few decades ago but till day concerned agencies failed in construction of the road. The residents are still living like an early man-age in this modern era of technology.

The killing of the Parihar brothers in Nov 2018 shocks the Kishtwar town over such a heinous incident and the general public from both communities comes across streets and seeks justice but politics once again rocks and tries to push back Kishtwar in 1993 situations only for their pity gain. The killing of the Parihar brothers was condemned by various social and political activists but calling each other anti-nationalist had once again hit back the Kishtwar. In the mean-time installation of bunkers in Kishtwar town was once a great threat to brotherhood among both communities as the installation of bunkers is for the safety of the public, but some miscreants are socially and politically raising the issue for their pity gain"

It's time to ask "Why is every upgrowing Political Leader or Social Activist targeted" as, after this killing, Source informed, that Mohan Lal Bhandari was one among those who were killed by unknown gunmen in 2006. Mohan Lal Bhandari was one of the hardworking socio-political activists who two times contest Assembly Election from Inderwal constituency was targeted and killed that raises questions again and again when it will be stopped and when will we move free across Kishtwar district. It was a time when Mohan Lal Bhandari was serving society as the best social activist across the Kishtwar district and particularly peoples of Inderwal.

Though it is worth mentioning that Kishtwar district witnesses various communal riots in the Padder area and in Kishtwar during 2013 where someone was set on fire and crores property belonging to both communities were damaged. But it's a matter of harmony and brotherhood, both communities across Kishtwar town fight against terrorism to save long decades of peace in the town.

In the kind of polarization that has been taking place and the warning signals that have been coming from time to time, it was essential for the state to take corrective measures. With Kishtwar's socio-cultural milieu, it would not have been difficult. There have been enough signs that everything is not lost there. Despite the vulnerability felt by Hindus during the period when selective killings were taking place, there was no out-migration at the societal level and the bonds between people of different communities have continued. That is the reason why it does not take much time to normalize the situation after each flare-up and why, between two moments of communal clashes, there is normal inter-community interaction. People attend each other's festivals and marriage functions and continue to have a mixed social life. Despite the earlier communal clashes, Kishtwar continues to have localities with a mixed population that is enough examples of people of different communities taking care of each other. Even as this family's shop was burning in the market, Muslim neighbors took upon themselves the responsibility of protecting their house.

Political Figure

Taking a look at political representatives of Kishtwar district from 2014, where Bhartiya Janta Party became the second-largest party in Jammu and Kashmir and formed a government with the People's Democratic Party headed by Mufti Mohammed Sayeed and later by Mehbooba Mufti after the death of her father Mufti Mohammed Sayeed. During the resigm of Peoples Democratic Party and Bhartiya Janta Party having its two Ministers in collation government including Mr. Bali Bhagat who earlier was having protocol of Health Ministry and later was assigned with a charge of Forest and Ecology department from BJP side and Mr. Sunil Sharma who earlier was having protocol of various departments including Public Work Department, Roads and Buildings and later was assigned with Power Development Department in collation government headed by Chief Minister Ms. Mehbooba Mufti. I would like to ask from Mr. Bali Bhagat and Mr. Sunil Sharma, that why Kishtwar road is in worse condition and who is responsible for a said cause? As both politicians are residents of Kishtwar and are affiliated with BJP among which one contested Member of Legislative Assembly election from Raipur Domana and other from Kishtwar Assembly constituency in 2014.

In this same collation government Member of the Legislative Council, the charge was assigned to Mr. Firdous Tak, who contested the Member of Legislative Assembly in 2014 from Kishtwar Assembly constituency on People's Democratic Party ticket and faces defeat from Mr. Sunil Sharma. I would like to ask Mr. Firdous Tak that why Kishtwar is not having better road connectivity and who is responsible for the loss of lives in tragic accidents?

"Since long from past several decades thousands of precious lives got killed in tragic road accidents across Chenab Valley as compare to lives killed in Kashmir during terrorism".

Besides these representatives from BJP and PDP, mass leader from Jammu and Kashmir National Conference Mr. Sajjad Ahmed Kichloo who became two times MLA till 2014 and was having protocol of Cabinet Minister in the resigm headed by Former Chief Minister Mr. Omar Abdullah and during said resigm, Kishtwar town came under the attack of communal violence that was later investigated by Commissions formed by that time of government. Sajjad Kichloo contested third-time Member of the Legislative Assembly election in 2014 and was later appointed Member of Legislative Council by party high command. I would like to ask MLC Sajjad Kichloo, that you became two times MLA, onetime MLC and Cabinet Minister, Why Kishtwar township didn't get better road connectivity and who is responsible for tragic accidents happening in daily routine?

Besides this mass leader from Indian National Congress G M Saroori became third-time Member of Legislative Assembly in 2014 from Inderwal constituency in Kishtwar district and was assigned with the protocol of Cabinet Minister in collation government during PDP, Congress and NC, Congress resigm and was having charge of various departments including Public Work Department, Roads and Buildings, Forest and Ecology, Education and various other departments. G M Saroori is a mass leader in the congress party and also having charge of Jammu and Kashmir Pradesh Congress Committee Vice President in Union Territory of Jammu and Kashmir. I would like to ask MLA Inderwal that you became a third-time Legislature from the same district, Why Kishtwar township roads are in shambles, and who is responsible for tragic accidents happening every upcoming day?

Besides these elected political representatives various other political leaders contested Member of Legislative Assembly from Inderwal and Kishtwar constituencies and are holding charges of District Presidents and are working for strengthening their parties on the ground didn't look back after their election results. I would like to ask from all contested Legislatures that why Kishtwar district roads are in worse condition and who is responsible for the same?

“Education in Kishtwar”

No doubt that the center and state governments have launched various schemes for poor students to avail themselves of benefits and receive an education free of cost in government institutions. These schemes are implemented through proper guidance and publicity through social and print media across the Union Territory. Mostly government is giving its top priority to Schedule Caste, Schedule Tribe, and Other Backward Class students to take education and increase literacy rate. As most of the students belonging to poor communities send off their studies as they are not having any source of income resulting from that illiteracy rate increases of such students.

Taking a look at modern education in the Kishtwar district, "No one can trust that what is happening in government institutions and what teachers are doing during their duties. Are students interested in learning lessons in class or not, why the results of board exams fall in the Kishtwar district".

Opinioning the fact of above said points, "That Kishtwar became the hub of political parties and politicians who for their gain do nothing in the modernization of educational institutions. Self-interested politicians opened hundreds of primary and middle schools to give benefits to their close party worker,s not to poors who was deserving the job. As the schools were opened through proper documentation and reports and those who were appointed as teachers through Rahber re Taleem or General Line rules accordingly. After the opening of school, these schools were club combined and teachers were posted in the combined school.

"A question arises that if schools were opened for providing basic education to poor and downtrodden students in nearby schools through proper criteria and guidelines, then what is the reason for club combining, was it only done to provide the benefit to their own party workers, Was the documentation fraud when schools were opened, who is responsible?

The poor and downtrodden public of Kishtwar is still unknown for the same. Being a citizen, I also applied for the said post in the year 2013, Not having a huge source of money and political protocol, the same criteria were changed and another one was appointed on basis of political influence. I am not against the same, "I would like to ask from every section of society, Was the decision of RET and General Line Teachers appointment done on justice or not", Why the deserving candidates were neglected?

Besides all these, I have inspected various schools across and particularly Kishtwar district, and see that mostly the schools are in defunct position and if they are opened only 1 or 2 teachers visit they're and perform their duties.

"A bitter fact and truth, that one who is a teacher of government schools seek admission of his son or daughter in a private school and told that private school teacher teaches well to students beside government school". Opinioning the fact I would like to ask them that Why you as a teacher prefers to seek admission in private school, you teachers having a source of income do so, what a poor father can do as he is not having a better source of income.

Happening so in government schools, students also didn't pay any heed toward their studies as teachers are not interested to perform their duties. In Kishtwar various school sans infrastructure and teaching staff in various schools of as concerned authorities didn't pay any heed toward this issue. I would like to ask that why representatives didn't take the issue of educational institutions on peak, why they are in deep slumber? If state government is paying crores of rupees on name of salary of teachers, why not they checkout their record of duties and schools. Resulting the same mostly the poor and downtrodden students remain illiterate and didn't get benefit of government scheme that were launched in modernisation of educational sector in chenab valley.

"Healthcare and Medical Aid system in Kishtwar"

Tall claims of Health Ministry to provide better medicare facilities at the doorsteps of every nook and corner through numerous State and Centrally Sponsored Schemes, due to the lack of doctors and even para-medical staff in the hospitals of Chenab Valley erstwhile Doda district including Ramban, Doda, and Kishtwar people have no other option but to travel 250 km to Jammu even for the treatment of common ailments.

The Health Sub Centers, PHC's and Trauma Centers in rural areas and particularly District Hospital Kishtwar is the worse example of the pathetic attitude of the Govt towards medicare facilities in these areas. The Jammu and Kashmir government running Public Health Centers (PHCs) and Trauma Centers in some parts of the Kishtwar in violation of staff requirement norms and operates these from rented accommodations with damaged infrastructure. As a result, these Health centers still operate within the same infrastructure as they had before opened in some rooms.

Despite having the knowledge of the poor condition of hospitals across the state and particularly in rural areas and District Hospital Kishtwar of Chenab Valley, State

Government vows development in Health Department, narrates its working style in public meetings and before State / Centre but reality differs to his fictions. Acute space shortage has badly hit services at Primary Health Centers where health employees and doctors are finding it difficult to cater to the increasing patient rush.

Chenab Valley lying on the bank of the river Chenab and is covered with beautiful lofty mountains and hills as its geography lies in between Jammu and Kashmir and is often known as the "AND" valley because there is inequality in the distribution of facilities in this region in Jammu and Kashmir.

"Right from the Freedom", People have to face a lot of problems right from the beginning and the Government often ignore this region. If we analyze the "Health Department" that persists in this region. It will be clear that this region has kept on the Mercy of "Almighty ALLAH". Being a resident of rural region Bunjwah I opinion the fact that there are some drawbacks that lie in the health department of the Kishtwar and need the intervention of Hon'ble Leuitatent Governor of Union Territory for smooth Health care facilities.

"Vacant posts in Health department", There are numbers of vacant posts in the health department in our state, especially in Chenab valley hospitals, that need to be fulfilled by the Government at an earliest. There should be more than two "Super Speciality Hospitals" with proper Infra Structure and accommodation in this region so as critical patients must be treated as soon as possible.

"Negligence of Doctors", Doctors are considered as the best Professional persons in the world. Before taking Medical Degrees they have to take a Hippocratic Oath, that they will save the life of their patients from the pain and despair. But there are few doctors who take full responsibility for this Oath as more prefer private practice more than their duty. They direct their patients to come to their Clinics as they have made a business of this "Pious Profession".

On 09 Feb 2019, eye witnessing the fact, that it was a very unfortunate day for those patients who were admitted to Kishtwar hospital as only a few students practicing there were catering to the rush of patients besides there was no option left to visit Jammu for minor ailments.

"Medical Facilities", Medical facilities are negligible in this region. The types of equipment used are of old age full of rust. Medical Aid provided by the government free in this region is alleged sold in the market by the authority members for their own benefits. Few patients and attendants informed that they don't get medical facilities at a government hospital as they have to visit medical shops for common medicines.

“Proper Transportation in Hospital”, There are few Ambulances available in hospitals, and in some PHC’s there is no proper arrangement of transport. The ambulance service must reach the patient on telephonic call as soon as possible so as the patient shall be shifted for proper medical examination. Unfortunately due to bad road connectivity most of the critical patients lost their breath before reaching the hospital. Pregnant women have to face a lot of problems while Parturition. It was a very unfortunate moment for a patient that an ambulance drops them in the middle of the road and that was later picked by a private van to Kishtwar hospital but after the referral process patient has to wait more than 24 hours for airlifting to Jammu.

“Negligence of Government”, The Health Minister and their Corresponding Authority paid little heed towards this region as the Ex-Health Minister hails from the same region. They kept for the Mercy of “Almighty ALLAH”. Doctors are not made responsible by the government. for the livelihood of the people. “Shortage of Health sub-centers”, Kishtwar comprises a large number of villages. Each village should have a sub-center for the cure of widespread diseases with good medical facilities.

“Sub Standard Drugs”, It is common in this region, even an “illiterate” person with any Medical knowledge allowed to distribute drugs. Most Medical shops sold drugs with no authority to control them. It is need of the hour to check the drugs sold in markets.

"Posting of Highly Experienced Doctors", In this region, highly experienced, honest, and dedicated doctors are not posted. They don't prefer to serve the people in this region. Most of the doctors manage their transfer to the comfortable region on the back of political leaders.

"Private Clinics", As mentioned above, Doctors prefer private practice in the region more than their duty. They direct their patients to come to their clinic for better treatment. They have made a business of this "Pious Profession".

"Shortage of Infrastructure", In Hospitals of Kishtwar, it is a common problem in this region, and the work on government plans are very slow over the past few decades, which clearly shows the interest of State Government and legislatures toward Health sector in Chenab valley.

It is important to mention here that peoples living in rural areas have to visit Jammu hospitals for common ailments as the current strength of staff, and accommodation of Health centers, PHC's and Trauma Centers it is impossible to run the same during late night hours. It is the time to take a strong note in improving better health care system in rural areas of Kishtwar so that people of this hill and faroff area take signs of relief.

"View Point"

Leaving aside all these political representatives and leaders from Kishtwar, why not young educated youths come forward for their genuine demands and demanded a "Better Road for Kishtwar and its adjoining areas". Having hub of such mass leaders in Kishtwar district, Opinioning the fact that all these so-called leaders are busy for their own publicity and are playing dirty politics with lives of many people of the said region resulting someone to became widow, orphan and breaking the stick of old parents.

On the same road that is known as Batote Kishtwar National Highway 244, having 110 km in length, I was shocked when I heard the news of a landslide at Drabshalla that had killed and injured the passengers who were crossing the other side of the road by foot. In this incident, a three months old baby died which was a ray of hope for their parents increases my shock. In another tragic accident in the Keshwan area of Kishtwar where more than 50 precious lives got killed when the driver lost control over Mini Bus and fell down in a deep gorge where a 3-year-old baby Adeeba receives serious injuries and lost her all family members, that was one of the heart-wrenching accident which I couldn't ever forget in my life span.

After this tragic incident and accidents that happened on Batote Kishtwar National Highway in the jurisdiction of the Kishtwar district, I see so many condolence messages of all these so-called political leaders and expressing grief and sorrow over such tragedies with the beavered families and demanding exgratia relief.

The continuous power crisis across Kishtwar district from since past 40 years and we are being told that hydropower projects in Kishtwar will make our area self-reliant vis a vis energy and we would be selling power to other states. We have been given false assurances that there would be job creation through these projects. All these false dreams are being been sold to the Kishtwar people by the authorities and successive Governments. Neither we became self-reliant in the energy sector nor could enough jobs be created in hydropower projects except some jobs for laborers. We are still buying power from other states and NHPC is exporting enough power from Jammu and Kashmir by plundering our natural resources. We have only lost and gained nothing that has destroyed our nature and in return got false assurances. At a time when Prime Minister Narendra Modi claims to have met the target of 100 % electrification across India in May 2019, 80% of Government schools in Jammu & Kashmir are still un-electrified. The youth of our state have not only been deprived of the jobs in these power projects but we have also lost our environment, water resources, and forests as well. We are the biggest losers. From the last 70years, only 22 % road connectivity was provided to Kishtwar whereas in other districts it is more along with per capita income.

I would like to ask all these so-called leaders, who for their vote bank politics and publicity are circulating such messages on social networking sites and on print and electronic media for their own gain. If you are having any interest in the welfare and upliftment of poor and downtrodden masses, you first need to awaken your inner soul to become a well human of society and come forward by providing a helping hand and fighting for the welfare of society.

"I am not against any political party or any politicians, But I am against those who are not having "Humanity" and are befooling poors for their own publicity".

A question still arises that Who cares for poors and Why representatives are in deep slumber? For the answer to the above said questions poor and downtrodden masses of the Kishtwar district are waiting and it is yet to mention that will they get the answer or not. It is time to fight for the cause of justice otherwise we still remain neglected by the State Centre Government, if not I then who, justice for Kishtwar people to meet the genuine demands at its logical ends.

www.ingramcontent.com/pod-product-compliance
Lightning Source LLC
LaVergne TN
LVHW050427160726
843469LV00041B/1264

* 9 7 8 9 3 5 4 3 8 9 4 7 4 *